★ **Aardman**

ROBIN ROBIN

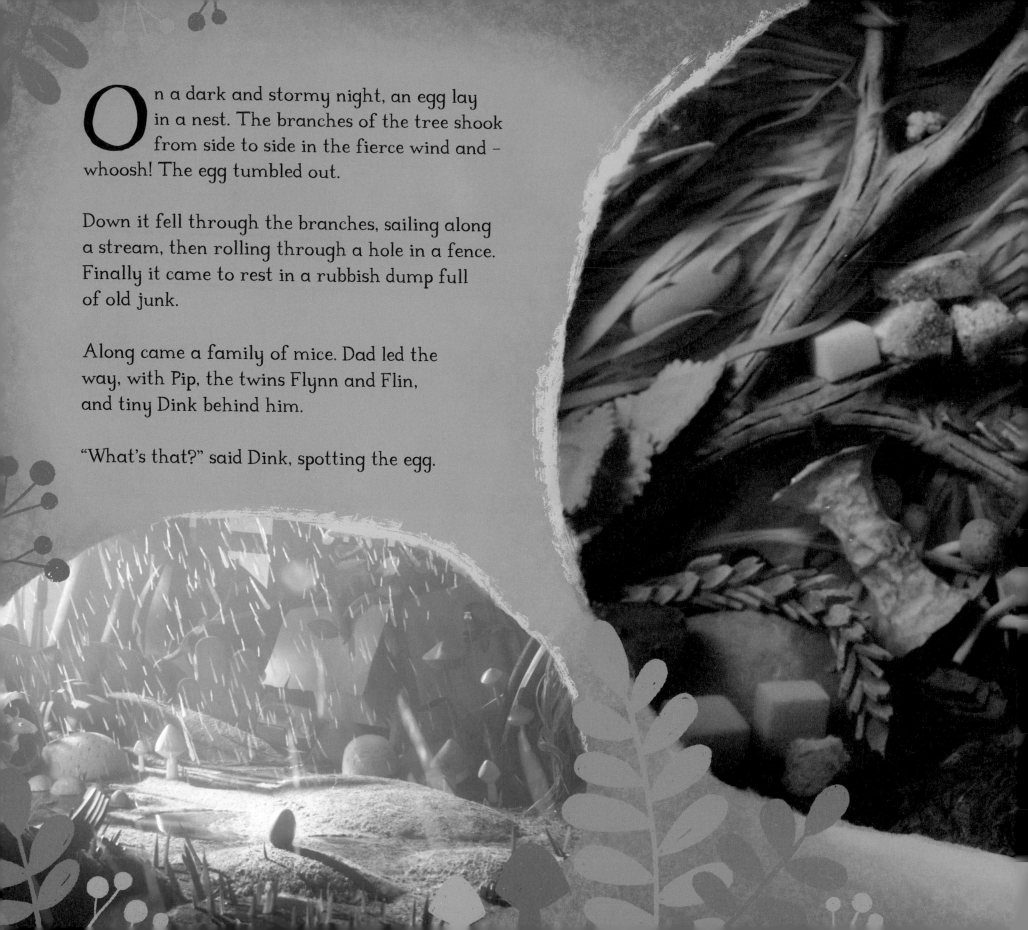

On a dark and stormy night, an egg lay in a nest. The branches of the tree shook from side to side in the fierce wind and – whoosh! The egg tumbled out.

Down it fell through the branches, sailing along a stream, then rolling through a hole in a fence. Finally it came to rest in a rubbish dump full of old junk.

Along came a family of mice. Dad led the way, with Pip, the twins Flynn and Flin, and tiny Dink behind him.

"What's that?" said Dink, spotting the egg.

The family watched in amazement
as the egg began to crack open.
A tiny brown head popped
out - a baby robin!

"Doodle-oo! Doodle-oo!"
she tweeted.

Everyone decided
that Robin should
become part of
the family.

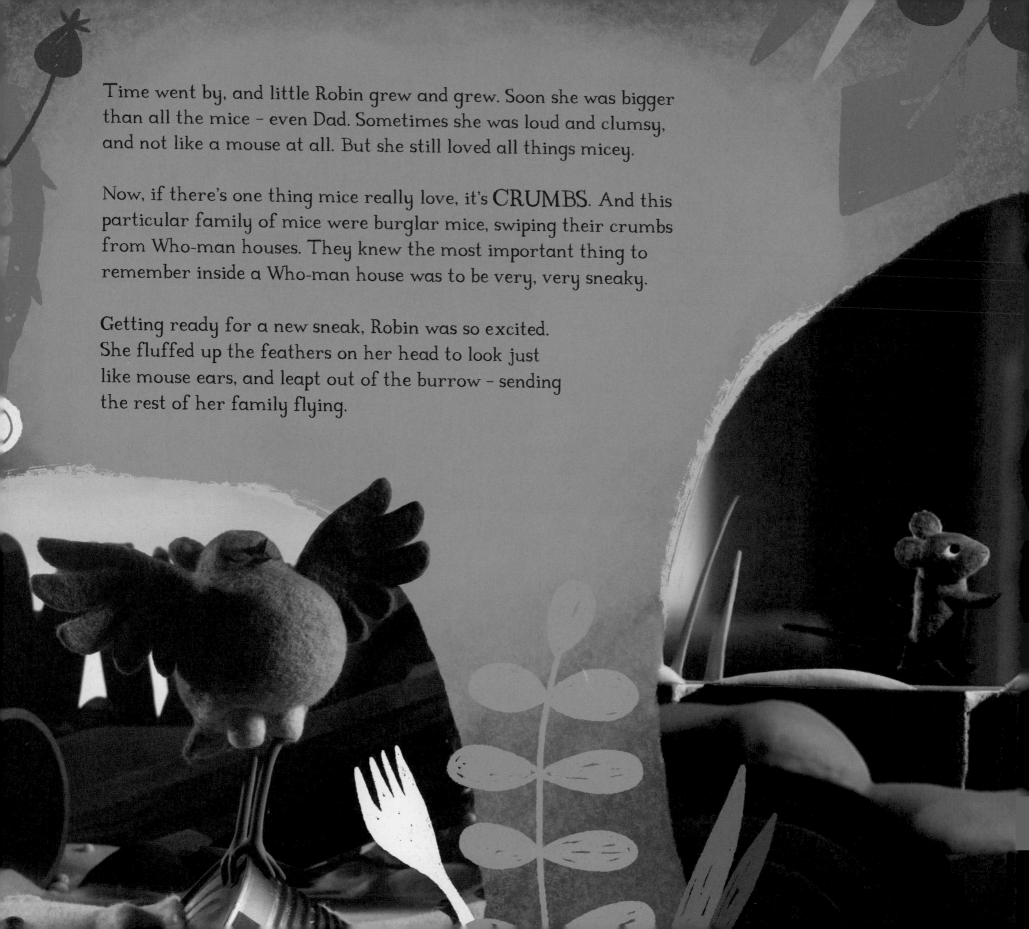

Time went by, and little Robin grew and grew. Soon she was bigger than all the mice – even Dad. Sometimes she was loud and clumsy, and not like a mouse at all. But she still loved all things micey.

Now, if there's one thing mice really love, it's CRUMBS. And this particular family of mice were burglar mice, swiping their crumbs from Who-man houses. They knew the most important thing to remember inside a Who-man house was to be very, very sneaky.

Getting ready for a new sneak, Robin was so excited. She fluffed up the feathers on her head to look just like mouse ears, and leapt out of the burrow – sending the rest of her family flying.

The family headed across the dump towards the Who-man house.

"We might find a pie crumb," said Flinn, hopefully.

"I'm going to get a crust," said Pip.

"Well, I'm going to sneak a whole sandwich!" boasted Robin, flapping her wings in excitement.

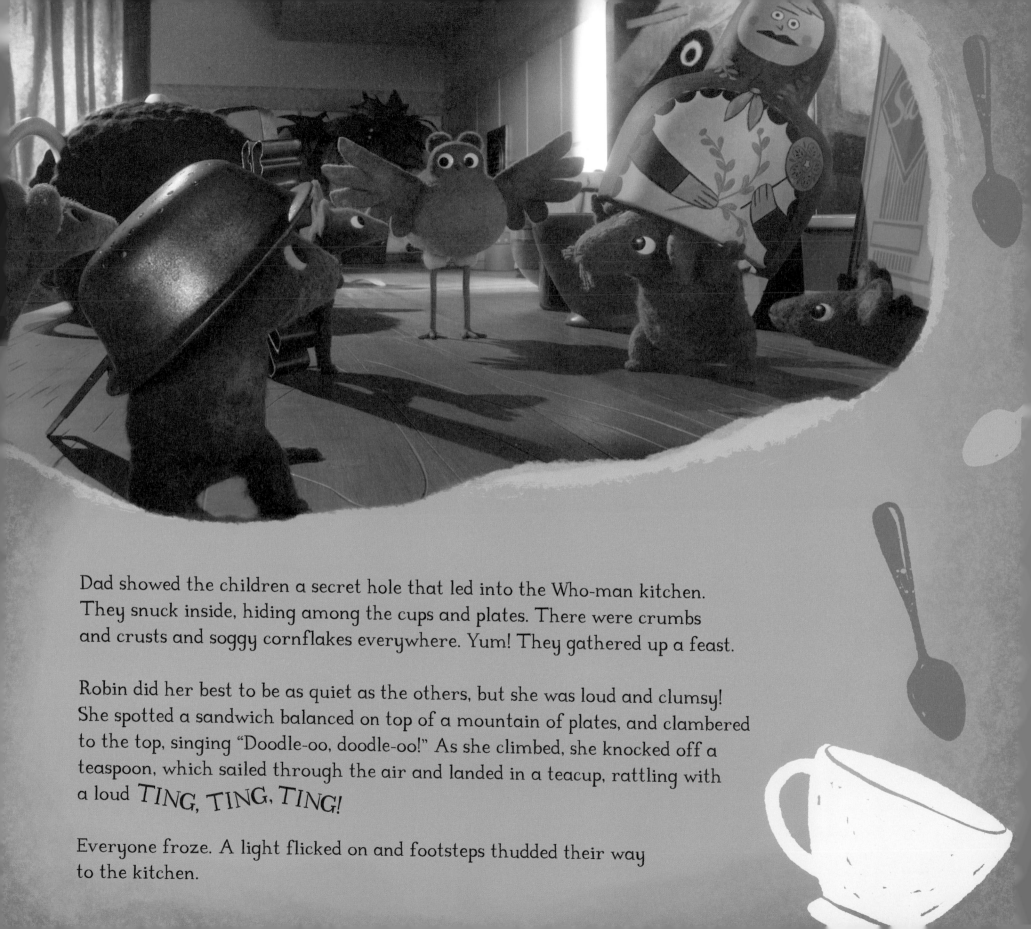

Dad showed the children a secret hole that led into the Who-man kitchen. They snuck inside, hiding among the cups and plates. There were crumbs and crusts and soggy cornflakes everywhere. Yum! They gathered up a feast.

Robin did her best to be as quiet as the others, but she was loud and clumsy! She spotted a sandwich balanced on top of a mountain of plates, and clambered to the top, singing "Doodle-oo, doodle-oo!" As she climbed, she knocked off a teaspoon, which sailed through the air and landed in a teacup, rattling with a loud TING, TING, TING!

Everyone froze. A light flicked on and footsteps thudded their way to the kitchen.

"Who-mans!" gasped Robin. The mice dropped their crumbs and they all ran for their lives.

Back at home, Robin felt terrible. Because of her, the family were still hungry.

That night, everyone was fast asleep – except Robin. She was thinking. If she could be the mousiest mouse, she could sneak into a house all by herself and bring back crumbs for her family. They would be so proud of her!

So off Robin went, into the cold dark night . . .

After a few wrong turns, she reached a shed
with a crack in the door. Thinking she'd found
the Who-man house, she snuck inside.

Two huge yellow eyes glared out at her.
Robin ran, as fast as she could – right
past a magpie, who had been digging up
a shiny bottle top from the snow.

"CAT!" shouted Robin, dashing past.

"AAH!" screamed Magpie. The pair
raced across the snow, the Cat right
behind them. "Fly away, silly bird!"
yelled Magpie.

"I can't fly," puffed Robin, as
they leapt into some brambles.
"Why don't YOU fly away?"

"I've got a broken wing!"
panted Magpie, glancing
back at the Cat with
an accusing look.

The two of them ran for their lives, all the way to an old tree. This was Magpie's house, and it was full of shiny things he had collected. Buttons, nails, forks, bottle tops – the shinier, the better.

"What were you doing in that shed?" asked Magpie.

"Looking for crumbs," said Robin. She gazed out of the tree at the Who-man house in the distance. "I bet they've got loads of crumbs in there!" she said.

"Yes, they've got loads of everything," said Magpie, sighing. "And all because of that magic shiny wishing star." He pointed to a Christmas tree glowing in the window of the house.

"Once a year, the Who-mans take a spiky tree, cover it in beautiful rubbish and put a magic star on top. Then they make a wish – and in the morning they get anything they want!"

"Wow!" said Robin. "Anything? Like CRUMBS?"

"Crumbs?" said Magpie. "Don't be absurd!"

"But . . . what could be better than crumbs?" asked Robin.

Magpie tutted. "THINGS, of course!" he said. "Things make you happy!" He pointed at all the objects in his collection. "If I had that star, I'd wish for all the THINGS in the world!"

Robin gazed at the Who-man house, thinking hard. "OK then," she said, suddenly. "I'll sneak us the star."

"Impossible!" cried Magpie.

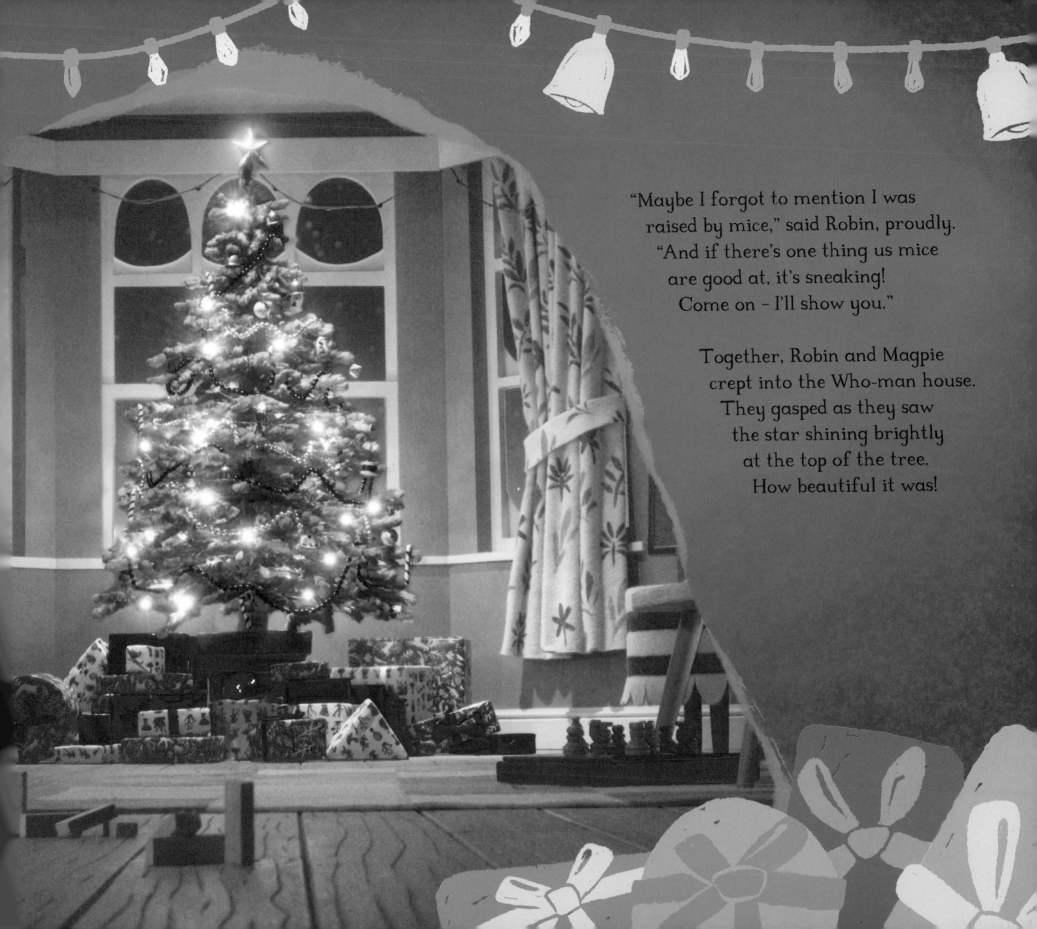

"Maybe I forgot to mention I was
raised by mice," said Robin, proudly.
"And if there's one thing us mice
are good at, it's sneaking!
Come on – I'll show you."

Together, Robin and Magpie
crept into the Who-man house.
They gasped as they saw
the star shining brightly
at the top of the tree.
How beautiful it was!

"Just do exactly what I do," whispered Robin, edging towards the tree. But even though she tried her best to be a sneaky mouse, Robin knocked over a glass of wine, got tangled up in a woolly mitten, and crashed into several rolls of wrapping paper. Magpie followed her, copying her every move.

At last, Robin reached the top of the tree and grabbed the star. "Got it!" she said. But as she pulled it free, the tree WOBBLED and the decorations CRASHED to the floor!

Above them, they heard the loud thuds of Who-mans waking up.

"Time to go!" exclaimed Magpie, hopping along a branch to a nearby window.

At that moment, Magpie lost his grip and the tree pinged backwards, whizzing Robin across the room towards the roaring fire.

"You need to fly!" shouted Magpie.

"Never learnt!" screamed Robin.

"It's easy! You just FLAP!"

Flapping her wings wildly, Robin crashed into a plate of mince pies, smashed into a lampshade, skied through a row of Christmas cards, and shot through the open window, grabbing the star and leaving a trail of destruction behind her.

"Woohoo! You're a natural!" Magpie shouted after her.

Clutching the star, Robin soared through the sky at top speed, crashing through the roof of the old shed and landing with a THUMP. A sly face with sharp teeth appeared in front of her.

"Why, it's the little bird who scrabbles around like a mouse," sneered the Cat. "Oh, those ears! Who are you trying to fool? You'll never be a REAL mouse."

Robin was desperate to escape. She spotted a hole in the roof and began to climb . . . but the Cat knocked her off, trapping her.

"You really are a terrible mouse!" said the Cat, closing in. "With NOWHERE left to sneak."

At that moment, a plank in the wall moved and Magpie's head popped through. He was holding a match to help him see.

"Robin!" he cried, seeing his friend cornered.

Robin grabbed the match, swinging it to push the Cat back. The match brushed against some nearby rags and set them ablaze. As the fire spread all around them, Robin and Magpie grabbed the star, dashed out of the gap in the wall and ran for their lives. The terrified Cat ran the other way.

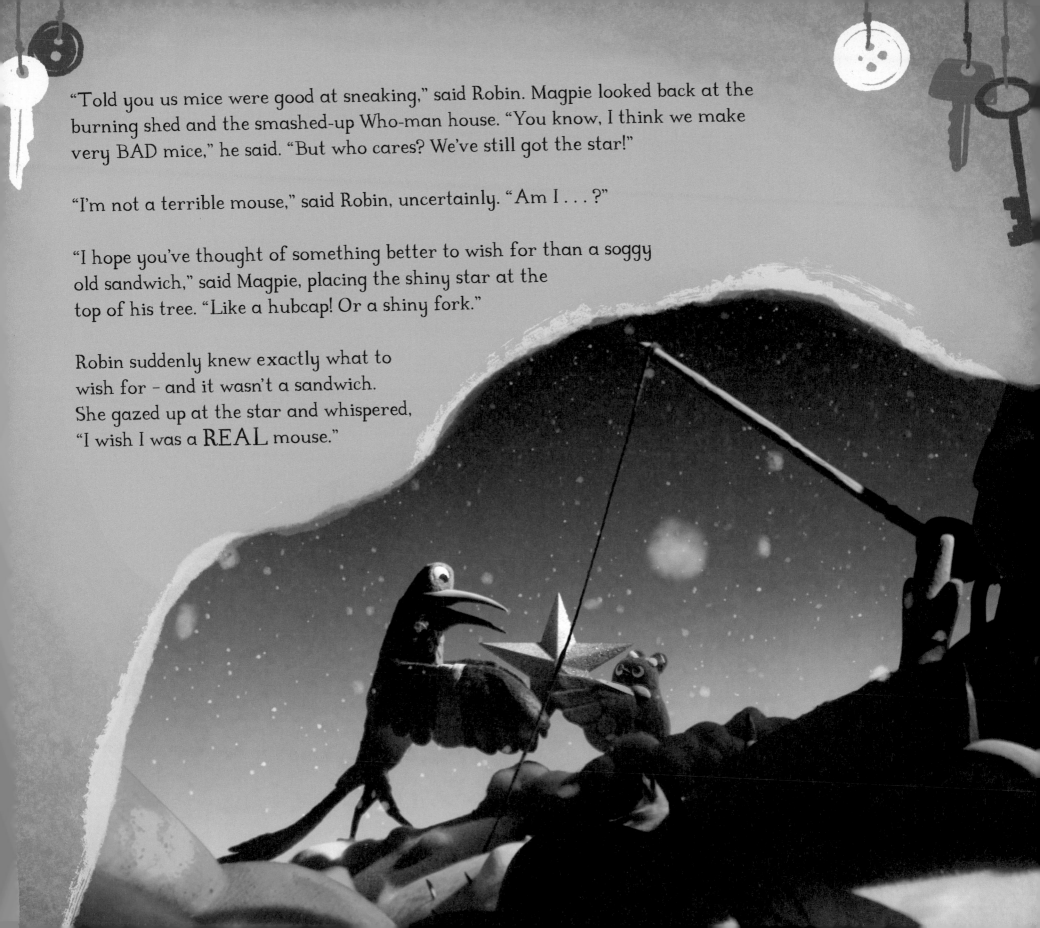

"Told you us mice were good at sneaking," said Robin. Magpie looked back at the burning shed and the smashed-up Who-man house. "You know, I think we make very BAD mice," he said. "But who cares? We've still got the star!"

"I'm not a terrible mouse," said Robin, uncertainly. "Am I . . . ?"

"I hope you've thought of something better to wish for than a soggy old sandwich," said Magpie, placing the shiny star at the top of his tree. "Like a hubcap! Or a shiny fork."

Robin suddenly knew exactly what to wish for – and it wasn't a sandwich. She gazed up at the star and whispered, "I wish I was a REAL mouse."

Morning came, and an excited Robin awoke. But her
wish hadn't worked - she was still a bird.

She shuffled outside to find Magpie jumping for joy.
A procession of shiny rubbish was making its way
through the snow towards him. His wish had
come true!

But as he ran forwards, the old tins and boxes
flipped over - revealing the mouse family hiding
underneath! They had been sheltering from
the snow storm inside rubbish from the dump.
The mice rushed up to hug Robin. "We've been
looking everywhere for you!" Dad cried.

"Sorry," said Robin. "I went to get us
some crumbs, but it all went wrong."
She looked down. "I'm a terrible mouse."

"I couldn't have said it better myself!"
purred a sinister voice. The Cat was back!

Running into Magpie's house, they were cornered!
The Cat lifted her claws to strike – but where
was Robin?

Suddenly, everyone heard a loud "Doodle-oo!
Doodle-oo!" Robin was standing on top of
Magpie's heap of bottle caps, flapping
her wings and tweeting as loudly as she could.

The Cat forgot all about the mice and
slunk towards Robin. The mice and Magpie
hastily made their escape. "What's Robin
doing?" whispered Pip, as they snuck out.

"She's being a terrible mouse!"
said Magpie, proudly.

Being as loud, clumsy, and unsneaky as possible, Robin flapped her way up Magpie's tree, knocking pinecones, twigs, old teaspoons, keys and buttons behind her to slow down the pursuing Cat. Covered in junk, the Cat followed the little bird out of the tree and on to an old, creaky branch.

"You really are a terrible, terrible, TERRIBLE mouse - with nowhere left to sneak," hissed the furious Cat, swishing her tail.

"Wait!" Robin said, looking at her wings. "I don't need to sneak! I'm a BIRD!"

Just as the Cat got ready to pounce, the branch snapped. Robin and the Cat went crashing down into the icy stream below.

"Robin!" shouted Dad. He was about to jump in when he stopped and looked up. Robin was . . .

FLYING!

As the Cat was washed around the bend, Robin swooped and soared through the sky. Magpie and the mice whooped for joy!

"Robin – you were marvellous!" said Dad, rushing up to her. "You're not a mouse . . . you're a bird, and that's wonderful. But we're the mouse FAMILY – all of us." Everyone piled together in a giant birdy-micey hug.

But Robin knew that her family were still hungry. And she had one last brilliant idea!

The Who-mans had just settled down for their Christmas dinner when they heard a "Doodle-oo! Doodle-oo!" Robin was at the window, jumping, flapping and singing! It was VERY unsneaky – and the perfect distraction.

While the Who-mans' backs were turned, the mice darted out from their hiding places in the shadows and filled their paws with crisps, crackers and crumbs. Magpie stood guard at the door and was delighted to get the shiny coin from the Christmas pudding!

And back home in the warm and cosy burrow, Robin, Magpie and the mice all settled down to enjoy a delicious, crumby, birdy-micey Christmas family feast!

THE END

SONG LYRICS

Learn the songs from *Robin Robin*!

THE RULES OF THE SNEAK sung by the mouse family

The rules of the sneak are simple and thus.
Follow them close, you could steal a crust . . .
Or a crumpet rind, or a pinch of pie,
Or the grease from the tip of a soggy french fry!

Crumbs and crusts and stale bread, soggy flakes and bin dregs,
Any old leftovers, we'll sneak home with us!

First, find a secret entrance,
Keep your eyes open wide,
For a hole or a crack, or a window with a gap,
Just enough to squeeze inside.

Once we're in, we creep around,
Tiptoe past without a sound.
Keep to the shadows, don't get heard,
Whisper every single word.

Last – the most important,
Remember in a Who-man place,
They're choosy who's invited,
So we must never leave a trace.

Crumbs and crusts and stale bread,
Soggy flakes and bin dregs,
Any old leftovers, we'll sneak home with us!

And when we're done, we disappear,
Nobody knows that we were here.
With crumbs in our hands, and warmth in our hearts,
And the sludge from a tin of a mouldy jam tart!

Don't make a sound – don't make a trace,
Keep to the shadows – take what we need,
The rules of the sneak are these!

THINGS sung by Magpie

THINGS! They make you happy. Things won't fly away.
Things will stick with you till the end.
Oh yes, on things you can depend!

See my bathtub? It's designer. Finest china – well, kinda.
Simply must have the latest bottle top. I love it so, I'll never stop!
This chair's hedgehog hair! Pamper climps? I've got the pair.
This is a limited edition piece of string.

I was a bird who couldn't fly – felt tiny while they flew up high.
Surrounded myself with things so gorgeous . . . felt enormous!
So afraid and so alone – things turn a hovel to a home.
Got no personality? I let my lampshade speak for me!
Hollow inside? You're not enough?
Just stuff that hole with lovely stuff!

Things are things that
make you happy.
Who needs friends?
I've got a shoe-chair!
No-one there for
you to care for?
Polish up your
silverware, for . . .
There's no better
company than
one penny!

A PERFECT PLACE sung by the Cat

You're a misfit, you're an oddball, you're a freak.
Micey ears atop a birdy beak.
But I've never seen a bird so peculiar, so absurd!
How about we play a game of hide and seek . . . if you can.

As a mouse, to me you seem to be just terrible,
Fitting in is more than dress-up and pretend.
If it's fitting in you're desperate for,
Come down, search no more!
I know the perfect place for you, my friend.

For you, I've the perfect place.
Not picky, stick with me.
What's in a name – a robin or a mouse?
After all, under the skin, you're all the same.
It's what's inside that counts.

Fitting in could be a breeze,
Just a squash and a squeeze.
Brush out those ears, come along with me.

Quick as a glug, you could be sitting snug, perfectly.
You don't fit in, but you'd fit in to my belly.
For you, I've the perfect place.

THE RULES OF THE SNEAK (REPRISE)
sung by the mouse family

Hey, over here! A song for your ear.
While we keep to the shadows, don't get heard,
Whisper every single word.

Look at me fly, catching your eye!

With crumbs in our arms, and a raisin or two,
And a coin from the middle of this sticky brown poo.

Look at me and you won't see my sneaky family!

Don't make a sound . . . Do make a sound!
Don't leave a trace . . . Do leave a trace!
Keep to the shadows . . . And to the light!
Take what we need . . . This is more than we need!

The rules of the
sneak are these!

First published 2021 by Macmillan Children's Books
an imprint of Pan Macmillan
The Smithson, 6 Briset Street, London EC1M 5NR
EU representative: Macmillan Publishers Ireland Limited
1st Floor, The Liffey Trust Centre
117–126 Sheriff Street Upper, Dublin 1, D01 YC43
Associated companies throughout the world.
www.panmacmillan.com

ISBN: 978-1-5290-7130-6

Written by Amanda Li
Based on the film *Robin Robin* created by Dan Ojari and Mikey Please
Text and illustrations © and ™ Aardman Animations Ltd 2021
All rights reserved. 'Robin Robin' (word mark) and the character 'Robin'
are trademarks used under license from Aardman Animations Ltd.
Robin Robin animated feature © Netflix 2021

1 3 5 7 9 8 6 4 2

A CIP catalogue record is available for this book from the British Library.

Printed in Serbia

FSC
www.fsc.org

MIX
Paper from
responsible sources
FSC® C116313